CRAGGER'S REVENGE

Adapted by Trey King

SCHOLASTIC INC.

ISBN 978-0-545-51751-5

LEGO, the LEGO logo, the Brick and Knob configurations, the Minifigure and LEGENDS OF CHIMA are trademarks of the LEGO Group. ©2013 The LEGO Group. Produced by Scholastic Inc. under license from the LEGO Group.
Published by Scholastic Inc. SCHOLASTIC and associated logos are trademarks and/or registered trademarks of Scholastic Inc.

12 11 10 9 8 7 6 5 4 3 2   13 14 15 16 17 18/0

Printed in the U.S.A.   40
First printing, May 2013

At the Croc Swamp . . .

Cragger is the new king of the Crocodiles. But he is sad that his parents are gone.

Crawley and Crug try to cheer him up.

SIGH

Ta-da!

Laval heads to the Sacred Pool of CHI.

Sorry, Dad.

Glad you could make it for the most *important* moment of your life.

You only reach the Age of Becoming once, Son. Today you become a *True Lion*.

I'll make you *proud*, Dad!

My son, for the first time, you shall take an orb, place it in your chest, and feel the power of CHI.

Awesome! I mean, for Chima™!

Suddenly, outside . . .

KABOOM!

The Croc escapes with Laval's CHI!

I've got to catch him!

Laval chases the Croc into the jungle.

ZOOOOOOOM!

Laval zips ahead.

Woo-hoo!

Drop the CHI, *Swamp Boy.*

Never!

The Croc looks for Laval.

Where did he—?

Haha!

Croc meets *foot*!

Gna!

Grrr. Lion meets *spear*!

CLASH!

The Croc's mask falls off.

Uh . . .

Now, surrender! Huh?

Cragger, is that you?

At the Gasping Creek, Laval is in trouble.

GLUG

A figure pulls him to safety.

COUGH!

A Legend Beast saved Laval!

No way!

23

Cragger returns to the battlefield.

How goes it, Crooler?

It won't be long before the Lion defenses crumble completely. Did you deal with Laval?

I . . . oh, no, Laval! Crooler, I think I made a terrible mistake!

I mean . . .

SNIFF

COUGH

I mean we won't be seeing Laval ever again.

Suddenly . . .

GASP!

Laval arrives riding the Legend Beast!

Holy Razoli! Is that a Legend Beast?

It's impossible! Legend Beasts don't exist.

They're no match for *us* and *our* CHI!

Cragger CHIs up!

Ahhhhhhhhhhh!

I'll show you what a *real legend* looks like, *beast*!

WHACK!

I believe *this* belongs to me.

Laval CHIs up!

Ahhhhhhhhhhh!

29

The Crocs all run for it.

Come on!

Let's get out of here!

You know this isn't over. We *will* be back!

And he's gone.

You could've completely destroyed him, you know.

I know, Dad. But the CHI gave me the strength to set him free.